Color My Fro:

A Natural Hair Coloring Book for Big Hair Lovers of All Ages

Color My Fro:

A Natural Hair Coloring Book for Big Hair Lovers of All Ages

Goldest Karat Publishing
340 S Lemon Ave #1077
Walnut, CA 91789

For more books, visit us online at www.goldestkarat.com

NATURAL

8
TEAM NATURAL

NATURAL

About The Illustrator:

Janine Carrington

Janine Carrington is an artist born in Toronto Ontario Canada who specializes in illustration. She was taught the basics of drawing at an early age by her artist father and continued her artistic education at the Etobicoke School of the Arts.

From high school she was accepted into one of Canada's most respected post Secondary visual arts institutions: Ontario College of Art and Design. There she spent five years working in various disciplines including: Drawing and painting, film and video, new media and printmaking.

Janine spent four years alternating between working and traveling to countries such as Japan, Morocco, Trinidad and Tobago, and most extensively Brazil. Janine is constantly updating her portfolio with pieces inspired by travel and work.

Find out more about Janine at http://janinecarrington.com/ or visit www.thisisyourlifestories.com.

About The Author:
Crystal Swain-Bates

A native of Atlanta, GA., Crystal holds a Master's degree in International Affairs from Florida State University and is an avid world traveler.

Crystal is the owner of Goldest Karat Publishing, a boutique publisher of educational non-fiction titles, coloring books and entertaining children's books aimed at African-American audiences. Tired of the lack of diversity in children's books, Crystal's goal is to fill the diversity gap in traditional publishing by providing readers with high quality books featuring characters of African descent.

Check out "*How to Go Natural Without Going Broke*", the picture book "*Big Hair, Don't Care*", and her "*Colorful Adventures*" coloring book line, all of which feature black characters with natural hair, promote self-confidence, and celebrate diversity!

Find out more about Crystal's upcoming works at www.crystalswainbates.com or visit goldestkarat.com.

Printed in Great Britain
by Amazon